Bugglepuffs and the Magic Key

by C.L. Bennett

ISBN: 978-1-4834-1029-6 (sc)
ISBN: 978-1-4834-1028-9 (e)

Lulu Publishing Services rev. date: 04/10/2014

To Jensen,

Happy Puahy

UBtt

COMING SPRING 2015

Bugglepuffs

AND THE MAGIC QUEST

FOR MORE SCRUMPTIOUSLY SILLY FUN &
GAMES ABOUT THE BUGGLEPUFFS GO TO

www.bugglepuffkids.com

BUGGLEPUFFBOOKS LTD PROMOTES
TREMENDOUS WORLDWIDE FUN FOR ALL!

www.bugglepuffkids.com

FOR

Amy
Connor
Ryan
Sienna
Sophie
Edward
Amber
Cameron
Beth
Alannah
Joseph
Millie
Betsie
Claudia
Izzy
Grace
Arthur
Oggie
JoJo
Victor
Megan
Jack
Benjamin
Ruby
Maggie

And all the other rascals I know and don't know…

This is a bit of Magic just for you!

CHAPTER ONE
THE TPOT TEA ROOMS

The adventure I'm about to retell took place some years ago after an extraordinary chance meeting with a very old lady with a curiously shaped walking stick. She entered the busy TPOT tea rooms in the little bustling fishing port of Brixham in Devon on a sunny Friday afternoon in the month of June.

At first she was hidden behind four tumbling towers of cupcakes dripping in chocolate butter icing, shortbreads galore, mountains of caramel meringues, and a scrumptious selection of lightly dusted jam cream sponges oozing Devonshire cream. Four light steps forward and she stood in full view.

The elderly lady wore a delightful, yellow floral dress; a big-brimmed sunhat with a pretty sunflower hairpin;

and eight long and intricate floral necklaces around her neck. She carried a soft, yellow velvet clutch purse next to her twisted walking stick as she moved towards the tables to get a better view.

The TPOT tea rooms had lemon yellow walls, jolly seascapes of Brixham port, giant pictures of delicious cakes, and an amazing collection of teapots hung from the ceiling. Traditional pots, stripy pots, potty pots, splashy pots, dashy dot pots, pictures of people pots, a Queen and a King pot, animal pots, cake-shaped pots, and a number that were terribly strange pots! There were giant teapots for twenty cups, medium pots, and small pots; but for a few lucky children, they could choose a teapot that was made of glitter or gold.

Below all these teapots were eight beautifully laid tables with every imaginable shape of chair! There was everything from ornate chairs to low backed chairs; wide sturdy chairs to narrow high-backed chairs; delicate antique chairs to swivelling, wobbly chairs; all with its own soft green, velvet scatter cushion.

The elderly lady beamed with delight at the silly muddled TPOT tea rooms and raised her arm to signal a rather flustered and overworked waiter.

"There's one seat left." Her voice had a soft tone.

"Over there, Madam?" The waiter moved disjointedly around the tables to avoid the customers' overflowing shopping bags and guided her to the one remaining seat next to me. "Sir, would you mind if this lady joins you?"

"No, not at all, please take this seat."

For some minutes, she sipped her peppermint tea out of her china teacup, spiralling her teaspoon around and around. She watched me like an inquisitive squirrel as I intently over-buttered my crumpet, dripping the melted remains on my plate.

Suddenly, her silver spoon crisply chimed on the edge of her cup. She lifted her head, and with a sparkle in her eye, whispered to me, "What are you doing here, young man?"

I glanced up from my over-scribbled notebook and half-chewed pencil, "I'm a trainee. A trainee reporter for the local Herald Express, and I'm looking for a story." I proudly stated. "My editor said, 'Go into the field, George and find us a story,' so here I am. Well, I've been in Brixham for nearly three days going from shop to shop, but nothing's particularly happened, actually nothing at all!" I sighed with a certain degree of flattened ambition as I looked down at my scribbled notes which read:

No.1, Story: a bold, oversized seagull stole a pasty from a tourist. Neither party were prepared to comment!

No.2, Story: a child locked herself in a sweet shop on the Quay while the shop assistant and mother had been chatting outside in the sunshine. The overexcited child then proceeded to eat her way through the shop for nearly an hour before the fire brigade had to break down the door. The mother and assistant were left distraught but the child roared, 'I feel sweet and fat and delicious!'

No.3, Story: a couple of fishermen had one too many beers and borrowed the wooden pirate ship model on top of the Maritime Inn, then tried to sail it out of the port.

"I suppose I could run with the child, or the fishermen, but it's not ground-breaking or particularly newsworthy."

"So you want a story – a real story!" She chuckled, shuffling for a tissue in her purse. After delicately blowing her nose, she pressed on, "Well, I have a story. It's a tale of wonder and enchantment. Would you like to hear it?" she asked, clasping her hands tightly together over mine.

"Yes!" I said, drawing my hands back and raising one eyebrow. Not even considering it was worthwhile putting pen to paper, I leant back in my chair to vaguely listen.

"This a true story about the Bugglepuff family and their fantastic adventures. Unimaginable magic and dangers, you know! Mystery lands and …" (leaning in closer) "and a key." She turned around to make sure no one else was listening and leaned towards my right ear, whispering in one warm, excited breath, "You know, you wouldn't think you could go on an adventure with a key, but you can!" She nodded.

"Hmm. I think I overheard the fishermen talking about them. Didn't the Bugglepuff family come from Brixham originally, but then moved away many years ago?" I questioned, turning my notepad over.

"Well, yes, they moved away but it was not so long ago."

CHAPTER TWO
THE FAMILY

The father was Captain Bugglepuff. He was a stocky, not-so-tall, rugged man with rather short, hairy legs. I think he rose to five feet, eight inches and a bit, although he proclaimed to everyone that he was five feet, ten. He had soft, brown, wispy hair that was beginning to thin and which randomly sprouted out in all directions first thing in the morning. He had the most electric, deep blue eyes, chiselled features, and a smile that brimmed over when he was surrounded by his family.

Locally, he was renowned for his exaggerated storytelling and relished recounting pirate tales the family had heard at least a thousand times; but with each retelling, they all kindly pretended it was a new adventure.

He was a crab fisherman. Every morning he left ever so early and returned in his battered, yellow fishing wellies for breakfast. His trusted companion was Trooper, a bouncy, black, crafty sea dog whose origins were unknown, except for the fact that he was found as a puppy by the Captain, whimpering in some discarded fishing nets near Berry Head. Trooper sailed out with the Captain into the roughest of storms sitting bravely on deck with military precision. Even when the boat tilted precariously to one side, Trooper still commanded the front deck and never left his post no matter how hard each wave battered his coat.

"A True Sailor of the seas!" Captain Bugglepuff would proudly remark to his weathered crew, but off deck Trooper was unfortunately quite the opposite.

He was out of control, always rummaging in the neighbours' compost heaps for goodies; and he loved digging giant holes between the garden fences and pulling all the neighbours' washing off the lines whilst chasing cats. He also pinched roast after roast off the kitchen table. This was the final straw for the Captain. He turned a blind eye in virtually everything that rascal dog did, but when a dog comes between the Captain and his food, a firm bellowing voice was required, "Trooper! Enough!"

Trooper knew that voice and would immediately bow and slope off quietly out of the way for a considerable length of time until he could safely return home.

Captain Bugglepuff loved his breakfast routine. Every morning he came home to an extraordinarily large bowl of porridge, honey on top, and four and a half thick bacon slices (the half slice was for Trooper). Food and Captain Bugglepuff was a match made in heaven. His passion for food was almost, but not quite, equal to his passion for his dear wife, Mrs Delirious Bugglepuff.

She had long, straight, dark brown hair to her thighs, a shapely figure, and hazelnut eyes. She was an overexcited bundle of enthusiasm for all things positive, from dancing to singing boldly (and badly) everyday no matter what got thrown at her – and a lot did get thrown at her! She dressed

as she felt, wearing brightly coloured, pretty floral fitted dresses which were often restyled by her daughter, Seasea, with knitted flowers and curtain frills.

On chillier mornings, she accompanied her fancy clothes with one of her four bold wrap-around cardigans, and a spotty or stripy apron. Her pockets were always brimming with treats for the children, wooden kitchen spoons, and useless bundles of keys that never fitted any door in the house.

She possessed many mad qualities as well and often in her rush, left emery boards, pencils, combs, or clothes pegs on her woollen jumpers while out shopping. Once upon a time whilst running furiously late for school pickup, she'd completed the washing and left a twizzled-up pair of fresh knickers in her hair. This led to an unfortunate period at school when the Bugglepuff children would have to listen to the teasing chants of their classmates, "Your mum wears knickers in her hair, knickers in her hair, knickers in her hair. Your mum wears knickers in her hair, all day long!"

Embarrassing Mrs Bugglepuff may have been, but forever a beauty to the Captain who first caught sight of her walking along the jetty while coming into Brixham port one chilly March morning.

Back then he was a young apprentice fisherman, learning his trade on the high seas and she was visiting from London with her only relative Great Aunt Bertram. Captain Bugglepuff and Delirious fell in love during that summer sunshine, and in the autumn, were married in All Hallows by the Tower, the Mariner's church in the City of London. They returned to Brixham, Devon to start their married life; and after a number of years, their family grew to four children and some remarkable pets!

Anemone, the eldest, and then twelve years old, was very sporty with platinum blond locks worn permanently in two long, waist-length pigtails. Her eyes were a soft blue just like the Captain's. She was a beautiful girl in both looks and nature and had a passion for the sea like her father, often swimming two miles each morning before school. She wore bright blue swimming goggles as a hair band and left them permanently on her head night and day because she always wanted to be ready to swim given the opportunity.

Her second passion was ponies, ponies, and ponies. Her dream was to have her very own four-legged friend. This was an impossible wish because the Bugglepuff family had a very modest, rented crooked dwelling between The Quay and Prospect Road in Brixham and little garden space. It had three precarious floors consisting of two top floor attic rooms with a leaky roof. The first floor had two bedrooms and a chaotic bathroom with a haphazardly flushing toilet. The ground floor comprised one modest kitchen, a muddy boot room and the Bugglepuff family were not likely to move any time soon.

Anemone did have one friend. A stripy, tabby cat called Tinks, who would follow her all the way to the shoreline and back, waiting loyally curled up in the sand until Anemone had finished swimming. Equally, Tinks was a super-lazy cat, pretending to be ill in order to sleep for hours; but when eventually awake, she was a brilliant and unstoppable mouser. Once the family took a short fishing holiday, and when they returned, Tinks was so furious at the lack of attention, she filled the bath right to the top with mice. Not nice that number of mice!

Anemone's brother, Compass, was ten years old with an athletic frame and short, combed back mousey brown hair and soft grey, calming eyes. Tidy and ordered in every way, he was a keen scientist and bookworm, investigating everything, and bringing home every injured animal he could find. He was determined to save the planet and all the animals on it. Compass dreamed of African adventures, Amazonian studies of tropical birds, and his best friend, Albert, his bold African Grey talking parrot went everywhere on his shoulder ... well, most of the time.

Albert was an exceptionally intelligent bird, but was also a parrot that had never grown up.

At thirty years of age, he had, at best, the intelligence of a four year old. He was exceedingly eager to please, but he was notoriously bad at flying and would usually hit something, or someone, to bridge his landing.

For one visit to the doctors with a sore throat, Compass had left him at home. Knowing exactly where Compass had gone, Albert had swooped down towards the Brixham surgery without any speed control at all, flew in through the doctor's window, knocking into a painting which then collapsed on top of the doctor's head. Poor Mrs Bugglepuff had to call the ambulance for the dazed doctor whilst she pleaded with him not to ban Compass (and his parrot) from the surgery for life!

"Oh, Albert!" Mrs Bugglepuff would say in exasperation.

While Compass was at school, Albert loved his weekly flight down to the Brixham Bakers, ploughing into a delicious line of sugared doughnuts, and returning proudly home with two in each claw for the children's tea. It usually happened on a Tuesday, so Mrs Bugglepuff always left a 'sorry' note with a pile of pennies in an envelope next to the front door in preparation for the arrival of the burly, barking baker! After Albert's visit, he'd stagger to the top of Prospect Road in fury, but would then be so warn out he'd simply take the pennies and stagger back to the shop.

Mrs Bugglepuff in particular, was frequently prone to losing the door keys but wouldn't even bother to look for them. She'd just ask Albert, and ninety eight percent of the time, he knew where they were.

He'd let her know by saying, "Sofa left," or, "Window sill, red curtain," but the worst place was, "Don't flush the toilet," and Mrs Bugglepuff would scream hysterically and race in a hot sweat upstairs to save the keys from being flushed away.

Mrs Bugglepuff was very proud of the affection and close bond Compass and Albert shared and would tell the neighbours, "He has such a magical touch with animals. It's like they know he cares."

Curiously different was his eight year old brother, Rocky, who had devilishly black, spikey hair, emerald green piercing eyes, and an explosive, competitive nature to match. "I can do this better than you," he'd boast, and a lot of the time he could.

Rocky spent hour's beachcombing, imagining shipwrecks, and dreaming about Captain Bugglepuffs elaborated pirate adventures. He had crafted an abandoned rowing boat from a shipwreck off Logan Rocks into a bed and spent every waking hour designing weird and wonderful treasure maps to test the family.

Mrs Bugglepuff would sigh in dismay, "Where's the kettle gone?"

Rocky would come out from under the red gingham table cloth, salute her and say, "Your mission is to find the kettle. Here is the map. Good luck, Pirate Mum!" With a willing groan she would go searching around the house until

eventually she would have to dig a very large hole in the back garden to uncover it!

Rocky loved to play practical jokes on his brother and sisters as well, and was loyally followed by his three trusty, fluffy, feathered hens.

Bolt was a large brown, fat-legged chicken with oversized feet, who would bulldoze through every treasure hunt adventure. On one occasion, she nearly lost her neck to a rather over-friendly fox but continued to stay close to Rocky's side as she swayed dizzily in the wind! She had fifteen metal bolts put in her over-stretched neck after that and would sit on Rocky's lap as his top hen survivor, pecking at his bulging top pocket, which was always brimming with chicken feed.

Snowball, a white, more refined chicken, laid beautiful eggs and comically assisted Rocky's treasure hunt games by scratching amongst the sand banks for the pirate's chest.

Haphazard was frailer in frame, speckled grey, cross-legged and an incredibly short-sighted hen, resulting in her being prone to frequent leg injuries during one of Rocky's numerous cliff climbing adventures.

He loved his hens and they loved him.

Last but not least of the Bugglepuff children was Seasea, a sprite of a six year old. She was very strong-willed, with golden, shoulder length curly hair, sparkly blue eyes, and she was always dressed in pink – a lot of pink! She wore pink frilly dresses, pink cardigans, pink vests, pink pants, pink socks, pink shoes and pink strings of beads, but always with a splattering of mud.

She loved the outside – climbing trees, dancing, fairies, cooking, singing, and making things.

Seasea's talent for needlework and knitting was exceptional for her age. She loved nothing better than spending a Sunday afternoon quietly cutting up her mum's wardrobe and redesigning Mrs Bugglepuff's dresses with curtain frills, buttons, or by attaching giant, crazy-looking knitted flowers. This caused numerous public displays of surprise and embarrassment, especially one day when poor Mrs Bugglepuff strode happily down Fore Street with some pride at the uniqueness of 'Seasea's fashion range' until a giant red poppy unstitched itself from the back of her dress, exposing her bottom!

Mrs Bugglepuff stopped abruptly in mid-stride at the sudden cold chill on her bottom, sidled up to the nearest sea wall and flushed bright red as she felt a massive hole in the back of her dress. "Seasea," she'd grimace in dismay and shiftily move backwards like a crab up the hill to the house.

Seasea loved all her family and had a strong bond with her brothers, allowing them to take her prisoner in one of their many adventures aboard the pirate ship. But she preferred to search out the hidden whereabouts of the chocolate box tin, which was filled every Friday afternoon by Mrs

Bugglepuff for the weekend. Seasea adored chocolate and would dream about what it would be like to wear chocolate clothes or to have a chocolate tree in the garden that you could go up to and just munch on when you felt like it. She would instruct Anemone, "As Queen of Chocolate, I would start my day with chocolate porridge and chocolate milk. I would then have a few chocolate snacks. Lunch would be chocolate soup, chocolate bread, and chocolate butter, and for tea, mmm."

"Well!" Anemone would laugh and say," I think you'd be quite sick by tea my dear little, crazy sister."

"No. No, for tea I would have a giant chocolate cake and I would have a chocolate knife, fork, and chocolate plate to help Mum. I'd eat it all then Mum wouldn't have to wash any of it up. "Silly Seasea," laughed Anemone who loved her little sister and her inventive imagination.

Seasea looked up to her big sister with great pride but looked down – literally – to something quite different. Her best friend in the world, aside from Anemone, was a short, ginger and black spotty pig called Polly. Polly was a confident pig with exceptionally long ginger eyelashes, who was convinced she was actually a dog. She'd sit like a dog, sleep like a dog, and bark like a dog. Seasea called Polly's bark, 'Woofunt', because it wasn't quite like a woof but it lacked a proper piggy grunt! She was a bit naughty though, and could firmly push the fridge door open with her strong snout taking a rather alcoholic trifle on one occasion, and

then spending the rest of the afternoon swaying stupidly around the garden in a delirious daze!

Polly pig had no desire to live outside and if she could permanently have her belly rubbed under the kitchen table that would be perfect. Seasea's weekly chore was to collect the hen's eggs and deliver them in a basket to the neighbours. So, Polly would 'woofunt' excitedly and trot next to Seasea who'd giggle and zigzag from house to house.

The neighbours would laugh and say, "What a piglorious pair!"

CHAPTER THREE
SURPRISE!

It was a gloriously sunny Saturday morning in early April. The seagulls were spiralling around the roof tops in Brixham harbour, when a crisp, white embossed envelope dropped through the Bugglepuff's letterbox. It had a grand London postmark.

The children looked intently at the letter because they had never received letters from London ever since poor Aunt Bertram had sadly passed away a few years ago. Mrs Bugglepuff opened the letter, and began to read it. "Oh," she said, "Oh Gosh!" she stammered, flushing bright red.

"What is it? What is it?" shouted the children in an excited chorus.

Rocky had accidently poured half his cornflakes across the table in his desire to look at the letter, but Mrs Bugglepuff was far too distracted and just scooped her apron out of the way and walked over to the kitchen sink.

"Mum, is everything ok?" questioned Anenome.

"Well, yes dear. Yes, I think it is."

Her eyes widened with excitement as she glanced at the children, then the letter, then back at the children in

blissful delight. The children for once went completely quiet, waiting for Mrs Bugglepuff to deliver the news.

Captain Bugglepuff had just returned from fishing and he caught onto the silence as soon as he walked into the room.

Even Polly pig lying under the kitchen table getting belly rubs from Seasea's feet didn't make one grunt.

Compass impatiently broke the silence, "Mum, what's happened, what is it?"

"It's Great Aunt Bertram. She's left me, us (she paused), a mill house down on the creek. It's got land and space, and, oh, a monthly income of £1234.56."

Mrs Bugglepuff was simply in disbelief and needed to rest against the kitchen sink in shock. Seasea and her bouncy yellow locks dragged a rocking chair around the table to get the best view of the letter. Seasea couldn't read complicated words but wanted to look important next to her Mum and see if there were any pictures. Captain Bugglepuff looked utterly bewildered.

"Gosh, m'dears, we've never had more than a few pennies in our life."

"In all my treasure chest dreams!" he cried pulling out his yellow and red spotted handkerchief from his seaweed covered, welly boot to wipe his watering eyes.

"Oh, my shipmates, that means a home for the children, for us, and for the animals! Our own home! And I can stop crab fishing. No more early mornings. Oh! How simply tremendous, tremendous!" He roared with a deep belly laugh and lifted Seasea up into the air spinning her round and round until they were both quite giddy.

Mrs Bugglepuff swept her eyes around the room and began to blub big tears of joy. "How wonderful," she sobbed, "How generous," followed by a bigger sob. "Dear Aunt Bertram, what a gift!" and she sobbed even louder.

Poor Mrs Bugglepuff was so distracted and in such a muddle, she caught her apron ties on the porridge handle and poured the whole warmed porridge pot over poor Rocky, Haphazard the hen, and Polly pig. They all laughed despite the mess and sticky goo and an excited chatter filled the kitchen like the magic of every Christmas rolled into one.

"So what happens now?" asked the detailed Compass, in his ordered fashion.

"Well, it says here, we need to be at the property on the thirteenth of April at 2 p.m. That's in only ten days! And there is a map."

"Wow, like a real treasure map!" Rocky's eyes grew wider and wider with delight as he wiped large patches of sloppy porridge off his scruffy shirt aided by Trooper, Polly pig, and Tinks, who gleefully licked the wooden kitchen floor spotlessly clean.

Mrs Bugglepuff beamed and cupped her hands to her face giggling like Seasea, then read on, "We are meeting Aunt Bertram's solicitor to sign the ownership over to us and it's no more than thirty miles from here. Do you think the car will make it, Captain?"

The Bugglepuff's battered blue Land Rover hadn't been used in nearly two years after the hens had taken to laying in the engine, and Captain Bugglepuff, being the softy he was, hadn't the heart to move them.

After a short pause, Captain Bugglepuff broke into a smile. "I think on this one occasion the 'ladies' won't mind us moving their home! Rocky, Compass, Anemone, Seasea, we have ten days to get that hen house of a car fully operational. Let's get to work, shipmates."

With that, the children shuffled happily into a pretend pirate line up followed by their trusty pets. Rocky broke the laughter by sounding an old cornet horn, and off they all marched into the garden followed by Trooper, Tinks, Albert, Snowball, Bolt, Haphazard and Polly pig who was still partially covered in warm, lumpy porridge!

CHAPTER FOUR
THE BEGINNING

The morning of the thirteenth arrived. A farewell chorus of seagulls filled Brixham Bay and the sea was glistening and calm like a mill pond. A slight chill at first light had turned into a warm sunrise, as the pretty pastel-coloured houses around the port one by one flashed with rainbow rays.

Mrs Bugglepuff had been organising, cleaning, and packing so frantically over the last ten days that in her organising, Polly pig had got a bath with Seasea, and Rocky got fed chicken mash for tea, while his chickens got his porridge oats.

Anemone could see Mrs Bugglepuff was juggling too much and had calmly taken necessary control over her brothers and sister.

"Rocky, Compass, and Seasea, Mum needs our help! One, two, and three, tidy, pack, and clean your bedrooms," instructed Anemone with a pointed arm towards the stairs. All three groaned but in an effort to look willing, they trudged up the stairs with Albert, Compass' parrot, flying headlong into a light bulb. "Oh, Albert, you truly are the silliest bird," laughed Anemone.

The boys shared a higgledy-piggledy L-shaped room with an aviary at one end for Albert. Compass had colour co-ordinated clothes drawers, neatly folded socks, and shoes in height order – trainers one end, stripy wellington boots the other.

His bookcase was exploding with facts and information sheets on wild exotic animals and an African landscape poster was stuck very precisely onto his wall above his neatly made bed.

Rocky, in contrast, had a giant pile of stinky clothes, muddy shoes, socks, and smelly underpants in the middle of the room, which he randomly dived into to dress, undress, and redress. For Compass, it took twenty tidy minutes to pack his chest; but for Rocky, it took five minutes followed by Anemone dragging him back upstairs to spend the next two hours repacking to a satisfactory standard.

Seasea had a shoe box of room in the attic with a leaky roof next to her sister's and had found an old crab cage for her toys, bundles of multi-coloured wool, knitting needles, button bags, frills, ribbon rolls and sewing box secrets. She carefully wrapped all her clothes between (well, you can guess) pink tissue paper. It was all very tidy and neat and earned her an extra bar of chocolate from Mrs Bugglepuff's chocolate box tin.

Captain Bugglepuff had followed his normal morning routine and gone crab fishing one last time before renting his boat out to an old fisherman friend. Victoriously, he returned to a house full of bubbling excitement.

"Well, m'dears, this is the day. In precisely five hours we will have moved to our new home!"

"I'm so excited," smiled a tired, slightly wobbly Mrs Bugglepuff.

"Yes, I can tell, dear. Why are my socks in the fridge and who put my bacon in the washing machine?"

"Aaah," Mrs Bugglepuff flashed bright red, "Oh, I have got into a terrible mess."

"Let's sit you down and have a nice cup of tea."

The Captain pulled the last remaining pair of rickety chairs out from under the soon-to-be packed kitchen table, ushered the children out into the garden led by Anemone and put the kettle on one last time.

The clock soon ticked on for twelve noon, the car was bursting with a chaotic assortment of family belongings. The trailer was six chests high with clothes, four chairs, one rocking chair, two stools, one table, six beds, two old yellow sofas, one battered wardrobe, one fridge, one washing machine minus the bacon, two bales of hay, one aviary, and a wheelbarrow with tightly strung together garden tools. Captain Bugglepuff, Mrs Bugglepuff and the children took a deep breath and squeezed into the car with all the furry, feathered, noisy pets. The car sounded more like a zoo than a family, but then a large family is not dissimilar to a zoo!

After two hours of snake-like winding lanes, overgrown blackberry hedges, potholes, and two rather abrupt engine breakdowns, one of which forced Snowball to lay an egg, the slightly smoking car with its precariously swaying load reached a little 'No Through Road' entrance at the top of a hill.

There were glorious blankets of orange and yellow daffodils on both side of the track, and partially obscured by a bank of bluebells, rested a battered sign at the base of a tree stump reading, 'Spring Mill'.

The Bugglepuffs cheered.

"Here we go! The Bugglepuff adventure begins," shouted Rocky, sounding his cornet, causing Snowball to lay yet another egg in despair. They turned the corner and the Bugglepuffs' eyes glazed over with amazement.

A steep, uneven, sweeping gravel drive led down to the most beautiful creek with a whitewashed stone mill house shimmering against the shoreline.

The meadows were glossy, green, and seemed to roll in a wave, as the Bugglepuffs overfilled car made its final descent down to the deserted mill. Spring Mill was slightly dilapidated and had seen better days but from that very moment, it took a warm, unexplainable hold upon the Bugglepuff family.

Towering high with an old mill wheel, it was covered in a web of fragrant wisteria and vines. Its battered blue window shutters just added more to the mysteries that lay within. There was a slowly trickling stream crossing under a cobbled stone bridge at the entrance to the mill.

The car lurched to an explosive, smoking stop by a magnificent old oak tree and the children, pets and possessions tumbled out. Anemone, Compass, Rocky and Seasea were running wildly in all directions, like they'd just arrived in a sweet shop for the first time.

"Mum, look! Look!" pointed Rocky. A large overgrown lake lay to the east of the mill with an equally overgrown island. "It's a pirate island. I'm off to capture it." shouted Rocky followed frantically by his hens.

"It's all enormous!" cried Seasea as she scurried around. Polly pig, trotting behind, had paused with delight at a weed-filled vegetable patch. "Woofunt, woofunt," scoffed Polly.

"Yes, woofunt, woofunt, indeed Polly. It's a magical home," laughed Mrs Bugglepuff as she enthusiastically attempted three times to hug Captain Bugglepuff as he desperately tried to prize himself out of the car intact followed by a series of sandwich crusts, chocolate wrappers, and a cube of cheese stuck to the base of his boot.

"Tremendous m'dears, tremendous," beamed the Captain finally standing to his feet.

But this private Bugglepuff celebration was short-lived by the arrival of a noisy gentleman rapidly descending down the little stony, hill track on a shiny, red bicycle. Anemone spotted him first.

"Mum, Mum! I think he's completely out of control. Look at the way those wheels are wobbling," and she was right.

He accelerated too fast and raced past Compass and Albert, who chose to fly up into the ancient oak tree for safety. The man was thrown in glorious fashion over a stone wall and into the mill stream with an unceremonious splash.

"Ouch!" said Delirious. "That's got to hurt."

"Oh m'shipmate, are you alright? Can we help you?" softly sniggered the Captain.

"Sorry, sorry, please do excuse me," returned a muffled cry, "One moment, p-p-please," and wet from the water, a bedraggled, sodden, rather flustered sort of fellow of about thirty years with a droopy, spotty bowtie, and very bushy eyebrows addressed them. "Awfully, awfully sorry. You must be the Bugglepuffs."

Dripping from head to foot, he offered a wet hand. Captain Bugglepuff simply raised an eyebrow and gave him a puzzled token wave.

"I try so hard to make a good impression, but frequently it seems to go wrong," the gentleman stammered, adjusting his now messy, soggy bow tie.

"May I introduce myself? My name is Mr Twigslowberry of Berrybemerry Solictors of London. I do apologise for my entrance. I was thirty minutes late for you and now I'm already late for my next appointment. So, if you'd like to sign the official paperwork, I must be on my way."

Clipped to the back of his now-damaged bicycle was a large white package with 'Spring Mill' embossed on the front. Twigslowberry propped his bicycle against an old and dusty wooden table at the base of the oak tree and in a frazzled state, unsealed the package.

Inside was a large pile of preciously typed paperwork bound in a green velvet cover.

Turning every other page, he offered Mrs Bugglepuff a very fancy gold pen. "Please sign here, and here, and there, there, and here. One full signature on the last page, and then initial three times here again."

Mrs Bugglepuff briefly paused, twisting the pen from side to side nervously. But then an overwhelming enthusiasm filled her heart and without any hesitation or looking particularly at the written text she signed away.

Mr Twigslowberry cheerily beamed, poured the water plus a small minnow fish out of his shoe, onto the ground, and cleared his throat.

Compass looked sharply at him, picked up the fish in his cradled hand and shouted, "Save that fish!" As he said this, Compass ran quickly and very deliberately over Mr Twigslowberry's big left foot.

"Ouch!"

"Maybe next time you'll think about all creatures and not just yourself!"

"Oh, err, yes young man. I do apologise," stuttered Mr Twigslowberry as his cheeks glowed red in embarrassment.

"Ah, I'm afraid Compass tries to protect all the world's creatures. That's his mission in life."

Noting his lack of popularity, Mr Twigslowberry dismissed any further small talk and continued,

"Right, now where did I put the other envelope?" Shuffling deeper into his bulging and rather wet, brown trench coat pockets, out popped a ball of string, two paperclips, a paper bag, one broken pencil, two toffee wrappers and …

"Hmm," puffed Captain Bugglepuff, rolling his eyes at Mrs Bugglepuff.

One thing Captain Bugglepuff lived by was keeping everything shipshape. Well, on his boat that was true, but at home he was just as disorganised as Rocky and more like a shipwreck with his belongings.

To relieve the anticipation, Mrs Bugglepuff comfortingly grabbed Captain Bugglepuff's hand.

"Let's take a wander over our new bridge to our new home" she smirked.

So hand-in-hand, while the children raced around the overgrown gardens and explored the creek, they strolled over the old stone bridge.

Two electric blue dragonflies met them on the other side; they seemed to dance in circles around them before gliding back to the bubbling mill stream.

Captain and Mrs Bugglepuff turned the corner and there was the beautiful creek, but what caught their eye even more was a very dramatic double gateway entrance. It was over ten feet in height and about eight feet wide. It had ivy and vines intertwined between its ornate, bronze frame but it stood alone. One twisted pillar on each side and nothing beyond it, just an overgrown winding track going nowhere. How strange and pointless they both thought. Not an entrance or an exit just a gate without a purpose.

"How and why was it put here?" wondered Captain Bugglepuff.

But just as they stepped closer, Mr Twigslowberry exasperated shouts echoed, "I've found it, found it, what a relief!"

Mr Twigslowberry was standing in an ever-growing pool of water, waving a smaller bulging white envelope enthusiastically. He handed it gently over to Mrs Bugglepuff.

"That's it. My job is done. Have fun Captain and Mrs Bugglepuff," and with that he was gone in a flurry of stones and dusty pebbles back up the track and out of sight.

Mrs Bugglepuff sat down by the mill stream on an old broken apple tree trunk surrounded by the Bugglepuff family's bright eyes and gave a great big sigh as she prized open the envelope with her worn out hands. Inside was a tatty green, moss-coloured velvet pouch.

"How strange," said a mystified Mrs Bugglepuff.

"What is it? What is it?" exclaimed the animated children.

There was an embroidered crest of an old oak tree on one side and the most intricately woven gold rope tassel tying the pouch together.

"Open it," exploded Rocky uncontrollably who was mesmerised by this mysterious pouch.

Carefully Mrs Bugglepuff prized open the pouch. A gold dusty mist rose from the velvet bag.

"Wow!" gushed Seasea.

Apprehensively, Mrs Bugglepuff drew out the most exquisitely large key you'd ever seen. Ornate and decorative, but also exceptionally crafted.

At one end was the most intricate engraving of a large regal oak tree with four tiny, figures dancing around the trunk. Its gold leaf branches were inset with four gleaming stones similar to a ruby, pearl, sapphire and emerald. Intertwining flowers were delicately engraved in gold down its hilt with a leaping hare and swooping owl. Looking curiously closer, Mrs Bugglepuff saw the figure of a horse tumbling in waves and starfish engraved at the key's lock end.

"Spectacular! Spectacular! What a key! It's really heavy, too," gasped Mrs Bugglepuff, whose hands were tingling.

"It's a treasure key!" roared Rocky.

Turning it carefully over, Compass made out three words inscribed on the back, "tempus vernum spiritus". At that moment, a sudden, mysterious warm breeze blew over the Bugglepuffs' faces and through the branches of the old oak tree.

"Ooow, intriguing," said Compass, looking around and then refocusing his attention on the golden key glistening in the sunlight.

"Mum, Mum, let's open the door. Go! Go! Go!" said Seasea bouncing up and down with her blond hair cascading around her shoulders. She never wanted to wait and always wanted to be first, just like Rocky.

"Ok. Ok. Let's go!" exclaimed Mrs Bugglepuff playfully skipping towards the old oak-panelled front door.

"Here goes nothing."

The key slid into the lock and it began to turn.

Mrs Bugglepuff felt her hand getting hotter and hotter and hotter as she turned it once, twice, three times. The door smoothly opened. Inside you could make out very little to start with because the shutters were blocking the light.

"Open all the shutters, m'shipmates. Let's see what we have here," cheerfully ordered Captain Bugglepuff.

Rocky, Anemone, Compass and Seasea, followed by all their animals, rolled into the house and went round in a frenzy opening one set of shutters after the next.

"Be careful, children," pleaded Mrs Bugglepuff as they all raced off at top speed up a darkened stone staircase with Captain Bugglepuff in hot pursuit.

"Well what's in here?" puzzled Mrs Bugglepuff. She calmly turned right upon entering the house, placed the key safely in her apron pocket and walked softly through a large archway. There was enough daylight to make out four window frames and steadily she managed to swing them gently open one by one.

The view of the creek was enchanting. It took Mrs Bugglepuff's breath away.

A wide stone terrace in front of the window had a direct view towards the mysterious gateway. But Mrs Bugglepuff turned smartly round, to see what this darkened room had to offer.

It was very large indeed. The whole ground floor at their old rented home in Brixham was now in this one room. A whitewashed kitchen with a double cream-coloured Aga sat at one end, and various fixed cupboards, copper pots, and a pair of walnut dressers sat against the back wall. There was an enormous oak family table in the centre, which could easily seat ten.

At last we can all sit comfortably round a dinner table together. How wonderful! thought a contented Mrs Bugglepuff.

Meanwhile, Captain Bugglepuff had followed the children up the stone staircase and was excitedly calling, "Delirious, dear, come and look, quick!"

The first floor had a long grey hallway, bare wood floors, and four plain double rooms about twelve by twelve in size. Mrs Bugglepuff flashed passed each doorway noting that they all had a bed with a stripy grey looking mattress, a sofa dotted here and there but best of all each Bugglepuff child now had their very own room.

With an extra stride in her step, Mrs Bugglepuff skipped merrily up the staircase to the second floor. A spectacularly large room with a vaulted ceiling spanned the whole of this floor with a porthole-shaped window framing a sparkly 180 degree view of the creek, and the far-stretching river Dart beyond.

"It's going to be sparkly. A perfect Bugglepuff family home," said Mrs Bugglepuff to the Captain. He wrapped his strong arms around her, shortly followed by all the children and Albert who swooped in and tumbled head first into Mrs Bugglepuff's apron pocket.

"Silly Albert," they all said as a babble of laughter and giggles filled Spring Mill.

CHAPTER FIVE
A NEW SUNRISE

The evening soon came and the sun was setting in magical ripples over the creek. The car had been nearly unpacked, the animals were all settled in the barn, and Trooper had finished his fortieth lap along the water's edge with Rocky and Compass, dragging seaweed up and down over the rocks. Seasea had picked the biggest bunch of golden daffodils from the top of the track.

Rocky giggled, "Look, it's a daffodil head on legs!"

Anemone smirked, but was far too distracted struggling with the final pile of clothes from the car. She blindly marched into the house followed by Seasea.

Mrs Bugglepuff was stirring the cooking pot and glanced over her shoulder to see a lot of clothes on legs ascending the stairs followed by an extraordinary bunch of flowers on legs entering the kitchen.

She smiled, "My little helpful angels." Mrs Bugglepuff scooped up the bundle of scented golden flowers from Seasea and planted a big kiss on her forehead, "Thank you darling, how lovely."

There was an old, dusty ship's bell conveniently hanging from the kitchen window, so Mrs Bugglepuff leant over and firmly rang the bell shouting, "Dinner time Bugglepuffs! Come and get it!"

The children raced in. Captain Bugglepuff nearly got squashed in the rush and Albert flew in with such speed that he misplaced his flight route, torpedoed across the dinner table, knocking out the water jug, and a basket of freshly made bread rolls before ending upside down in a fruit bowl with his beak stuck in a banana.

"Really, Albert!" laughed Compass and helped his flustered friend back onto his shoulder.

A noisy chorus sat round the table, clanking glasses, scrapping plates and dropping forks. It was a medley of chaotic family feasting; and with all their tummies full of a hearty beef stew and homemade bread and butter, they crawled up to bed for a well-deserved rest. Mrs Bugglepuff tucked them into their makeshift beds, glanced at their bare walls and said to them one by one,

"Tomorrow will be an exciting new adventure, I'm sure. Now sleep well and dream about how you'd like us to decorate your new bedroom tomorrow."

"Yes, Mum," they all yawned, giving Mrs Bugglepuff one final hug before falling into four blissful sleeps.

Morning came quicker than the Captain or Mrs Bugglepuff imagined.

The sun was streaming through their beautiful bedroom's porthole window. Mrs Bugglepuff was the first to stir from her warm comforting slumber. She began to gently open her eyes and slowly look around. There before her was the porthole window. She smiled contentedly.

But then she blinked and blinked again. The room had changed, or more dramatically, had been transformed.

It was now exquisitely furnished with floral tapestries on the walls, rich golden drapes around each window and their bed was enormous.

The Captain and Mrs Bugglepuff now lay in a luxurious four poster bed made of walnut wood with beautifully engraved flowers along the headboard and tapestry curtains hanging down each of the four sides. Wow, it was her dream bed!

The floor was littered with fine Persian rugs, ornate bedside tables, and exotic gold lamps sat proudly on either side of the bed. Landscape oil paintings, peculiarly shaped vases, quirky ornaments, and everything Mrs Bugglepuff had dreamt about in her sleep now filled the room.

"Oh my, bless my soul! My dream has come to life."

She wasn't sure whether to smile or cry, to wake Captain Bugglepuff, or just sit there taking in the new luxurious bedroom interior. She was in a befuddled puzzlement.

"Goodness me, next I'll be seeing fairies!"

"Welcome dear Mrs Bugglepuff," and hovering in front of her were four tiny children, no bigger than Mrs Bugglepuff's hand, floating about at the end of the bed.

There were two scruffy looking boys, one in cargo trousers, and the other wearing ripped, muddy brown shorts. Both sat cross legged in the air.

Whilst two twin girls, one with crazy curly blond hair in silver dungarees, and her sister with crazy curly brown hair in a navy blue pebble-edged dungarees, enthusiastically started waving and smiling back at the rapidly going mad Mrs Bugglepuff. All four wore identical gold lace-up ankle boots that glowed as they hovered. Mrs Bugglepuff's hands were beginning to shake nervously.

"Mrs Bugglepuff, my name is Puffin and we're not fairies," she blasted tumbling up the bed with her crazy, curly brown hair and sparkly dungarees.

"You're not?" stuttered Mrs Bugglepuff, drawing the bed sheets up around her neck.

"No, fairies are smaller, silly little things! We have no wings just fancy golden boots that float us around, we are the Guardians of Spring Mill and the Spring key. I am the Water Guardian. We have been waiting for your arrival for a very long time. This is my sister, Skylark, hic, hic."

Skylark was taller and faster than Puffin and moved gracefully up the bed to Mrs Bugglepuff's side. "You'll have

to excuse my hiccupping sister. She always hiccups when she meets people for the first time. I am the Weather Guardian and these are my two brothers, Nutter and Magpie, the Guardians of the Earth and Nature."

Puffin signalled to her untidy brothers, "Go ahead boys, hic."

They both lifted their caps and sharply moved up the bed. Nutter wore a tatty grey leather cap, and Magpie had a safari hat with a black and white feather.

Nutter lifted his cap and bowed, "Yep, good day to you Mrs Bugglepuff. Apologise for the shock of waking you like this but it's better now than a more unexpected introduction in the garden where you could run away! Sorry for my grubby knees but I look after all things to do with the Earth. Super messy job, but super fantastic!" he said as he continued to drop tiny chunks of mud all over the bed sheets.

Mrs Bugglepuff raised both worried eyebrows. She could see distinct similarities between her own rascally Rocky in Nutter's messy behaviour.

"We're supposed to be trying to make a good impression on the family," blustered Magpie, "Now I'm truly honoured you've finally arrived, Mrs Bugglepuff, and we are delighted to guide your way."

"Your way, I mean, my way?" Mrs Bugglepuff gulped and suddenly threw the covers over her head to take deep breaths, whimpering quietly to herself.

"Now look what you've done," grumbled Magpie.

"Me? What I've done?" barked Nutter.

"Boys, boys do behave!" scolded Skylark and Puffin blowing their cheeks out and peering down at the shaking, white sheets.

Mrs Bugglepuff peaked out hoping everything had returned to normal but nothing had changed, so, again, she threw the covers back over the top of herself in a frazzled state mumbling,

"I'm asleep, that's all. I must be dreaming. Over-tired obviously and so many changes. It's all too much for me. Now pull yourself together, Delirious, and take a deep breath, in and out, in and out."

For some minutes the sheets blew up and down as Mrs Bugglepuff calmed herself. Then slowly, she lifted the covers off her face to review the situation. But there were Skylark, Puffin, Nutter and Magpie still hovering over her bed. She hesitated, "You're not going to disappear, are you?"

"No," they smirked.

"You're not a figment of my imagination either, are you?"

"No," they smirked again.

Her cheeks flushed and she now took comfort from the deeply sleeping Captain next to her and began rocking his shoulders.

"Captain, Captain, I don't mean to concern you but could you please open your eyes? Now would be good!"

"What is it, Delirious? Winds a-blowing, south, south west by north, north east! Pull up the anchor and full steam ahead. There, there Trooper, good boy, good seadog," and he turned over snoring loudly still deep asleep.

"WAKE UP YOU CRAZY CAPTAIN. We're not on your boat. We're not at sea. And I'm not your trusted seadog. This is an SOS call. Wake up!"

"What? What? What's the matter?" A blurry eyed, slightly more alert Captain opened one eye. Puffin darted across and continued to hiccup on Mrs Bugglepuff's left shoulder.

"You see," she sighed.

"I'm not dreaming am I?" he pressed.

"No, but am I?" hesitated Mrs Bugglepuff.

The Captain shook his head, maybe two or three times then looked at his pocket watch next to the bed.

"Time, 7:39 a.m. Suns up. No crab fishing today because we've moved house. And I've retired," he sighed contentedly.

Then he sat up sharply and reopened both eyes to look at Mrs Bugglepuff's shoulder.

"Good morning, Captain Bugglepuff. It's a pleasure to meet you, too, hic, hic," giggled Puffin.

"Err, you, too," stammered Captain Bugglepuff. Even in his shock he still had excellent manners.

"So um, my dear Delirious, this is a bit different."

"Yes," interrupted Nutter and Magpie. "It's all going to be very different from now on."

Captain Bugglepuff shook his head and rubbed his forehead, "Hmm, this is going to be quite a strange day with four miniature fairies on the bed!"

"Fairies, we're not fairies!" corrected a chuckling Magpie.

"No, they're not fairies. They have no wings just golden boots. They are the Guardians of Spring Mill and the Spring key," confirmed a more controlled Mrs Bugglepuff.

"Oh, super boots. How tremendous!" coughed the Captain as he properly looked around the bedroom for the very first time.

After a few minutes of inspection, the Captain glanced down at his bedside table. There on the floor was the most comfortable-looking pair of what could only be described as 'posh' navy blue velvet slippers with a soft fleece lining

and the initials 'CB' delicately embroidered in gold thread. "Oh, CB? CB? Captain Bugglepuff. Are these for me?" eye-spied the Captain with a winning grin.

"Yes," laughed Nutter, crossing his arms and flying headlong into the Captain's crazy morning hair. "Yes. Yes, they are! Well done and …"

But Skylark swiftly interrupted, "Did you read the last page of the house deeds properly?"

"Oh, yes! Well, no! Well, yes! Well, no. Not really, why?" said Mrs Bugglepuff in disarray.

"Should I have?" puffed Mrs Bugglepuff fearfully, biting her lower lip.

"Yes, yes, it was really, yes, really, really important!" confirmed Nutter and Magpie.

"See, we should have told them last night and introduced ourselves last night. Not this morning when it's too late!" blurted Puffin.

"Too late, what's too late?" bleated Mrs Bugglepuff.

Nutter and Magpie tumbled off returning sheepishly with the deeds to Spring Mill. Mrs Bugglepuff turned to the last page and read;

Dear Mrs Delirious Bugglepuff,
You have been bestowed the gift of Spring Mill and the Keeper of the Spring key. This holds the power to the elements that flow through the river Dart to the out side world.

Be sure to keep the key in your possession at all times and we will do the rest and as a gift from the Guardians on your first night what ever you all dream will come true. Sincere felicitations, Guardians of the River Dart.

Skylark, Puffin, Magpie, Nutter
Keepers pledge,

"Oops, I didn't read this in advance and I've already signed it," winced Mrs Bugglepuff.

Turning swiftly to the Captain she questioned, "And what did you dream about?"

He paused and thought, and thought some more, and then with a worried comical frown muttered, "Oh dear, oh dear, oh dear! Ooooh tremendous! I think I might need to go and look in the kitchen."

Sensing the new confusion in Mrs Bugglepuff's frown, Skylark, Puffin, Nutter and Magpie decided to swiftly scoot off to the garden. Their presence had been more than enough for one morning.

"We'll see you later, good day to you Captain and Mrs Bugglepuff. If you need us just call."

"Same to you m' little shipmates," said the jolly Captain who had started to laugh and laugh.

"How charming, quite charming. Don't you think, dear?" hummed the distracted Captain.

"Charming!" shrieked Mrs Bugglepuff.

"Oh heavens above, the children!" and in a terrible panic she leaped out of bed.

Alarm bells were ringing in Mrs Bugglepuff's ears as she frantically placed two odd socks on her feet, threw on a spotty dotty dress, tied her apron back to front with the safely stowed key in the pocket. She stuck a wooden spoon in the back of her hair and with one last fearful glance back at the highly amused Captain sped along the corridor and down the stairs to where the children slept.

CHAPTER SIX
PIRATES GALORE

Rocky and Compass were notoriously good at sleeping in, unlike Anemone and Seasea who were always up at the crack of dawn but for some reason this morning none of them had stirred.

Mrs Bugglepuff tried to compose herself as she stepped down to the first floor landing. She wondered what the children's rooms were now like. Did their rooms get transformed just like hers? But more importantly were they all safe? As she turned down the stone stairs to the first floor, she knew straight away nothing was normal any more. The first floor hallway was an electrifying, brilliant yellow colour with brass ship lights and a muddle of antique wall clocks and cuckoo clocks randomly hung on both walls. There were over eighty in total. They created a beautiful hum of tick, tick, ticking in the hallway.

A rich, sumptuous broad tapestry runner ran the full length of the children's hallway embroidered with pirate scenes, castles, seascapes, tropical forests, horses, and wild safari animals. Mrs Bugglepuff pondered over it admiringly.

"It's as if the children have designed this in their sleep. Oh, but they have, they have!" She gasped clasping her hands over her mouth.

Mrs Bugglepuff's eyes saw a flash of coloured lights on the right hand side of the hall. Rocky's bedroom door was wider and ablaze with colour. She was not a materialistic woman, but this door was magnificent. It was made from a deep, heavy shipping timber with jewel upon jewel inset into the old wood panelling. She touched it, "Wow. Are these real?"

The door knob was made of battered old gold coins, the currency was undecipherable but the weight of the gold could be felt as Mrs Bugglepuff firmly clasped the knob and took a deep breath as she opened his bedroom door. Mrs Bugglepuff couldn't believe what she was seeing. She nearly fell over in utter shock.

From a plain white double bedroom the night before, the room was now twenty feet long and possessed a ceiling height reaching thirty feet. The floor had dropped by two feet and there was a heavy, roped gang plank. A slightly salty smell hung in the air which was not unusual around Rocky's smelly belongings at their old home, but this time it was more of a soft, salty scent intermixed with earthy sandalwood from the wide, gleaming oak floorboards.

Every wall was wood panelled with various closed hatches and trap doors storing games, books, clothes, and all sorts of undiscovered mysteries. A variety of oddly shaped maritime lights randomly swung and flickered in this magical new room.

The wooden floor joists had eight thick glass portholes set into them. A large pirate's chest, and a curiously shaped table, with a burgundy leather buttoned Captain's chair also furnished this mysterious and enchanted room. But where was Rocky? Where was Rocky? A large pair of twenty foot high elaborate, blue and gold seascape curtains screened off the far end corner.

Mrs Bugglepuff tiptoed across the floor towards them. One-by-one, floor glass portholes began to light up making poor Mrs Bugglepuff jump in surprise.

"Oh dear, stay calm Delirious. Your mission is to find Rocky, deep breaths." Jewels and booty treasure chests fit for a pirate king glowed beneath the glass.

Then suddenly, *"AAAAAAHH,* What on earth is that?" shrieked Mrs Bugglepuff, leaping up in the air. There, between her legs, under a porthole, was a squirming octopus two feet across, with dark, bulging eyes looking up at her with its tentacles spiralling in circles towards her. "Oh dear Rocky, what a shock!"

Mrs Bugglepuff faltered for a second while considering how exactly one feeds a new pet octopus.

"Goodness me! Rocky couldn't be a normal boy and dream about having a pet hamster or guinea pig. No, he had to go and dream about a pet octopus. A pet octopus! I will have something to say to those Guardians when I see them next."

But the thought was squashed, as all she wanted to know was where Rocky was and what was behind the curtains.

With a mighty swoosh, she pulled the curtains aside and there was a magnificent oak replica of a pirate galleon over ten feet long, with portholes, canons and a gleaming anchor. Golden steps lead up to the deck, with a glorious mast and sails flying the pirate flag, and there on the deck was an emperor-sized bed with four telescope bedsteads at each corner. Draped over the bed was a velvet, sea blue and green quilt glittering with gem stones and snuggled into crisp white sheets was Rocky soundly sleeping in full pirate attire, and, of course, a fancy pirate hat!

A strange old worn map hung against Rocky's back bedroom wall, Spring Mill was detailed at the bottom, but Mrs Bugglepuff preferred to turn and survey Rocky's magical imagination. She proudly smiled stroked his cheek and pulled the quilt up closer round him placing his pirate hat gently on his pillow. He stirred a fraction but then continued to sleep on.

Maybe, she thought, *it's better if he sleeps in a bit while I investigate the other bedrooms.*

So she proudly turned, stepped down the gleaming galleon steps, crossed the porthole floor, avoiding the octopus, and up the gang plank leaving the door just a little ajar so he knew he was still at home.

CHAPTER SEVEN
PINK AND PRETTY

Seasea had the next room along. Last night it had four pealing, yellow wallpaper walls and a chipped metal bedframe that wobbled when little Seasea had climbed into have her first night sleep.

This morning the door frame was now hand-engraved with castle turrets, beautiful princesses and dancing ballerinas. But wait, what was that smell? Mrs Bugglepuff sniffed the door.

"Cocoa. It's chocolate! It's made of chocolate. The whole door is a solid door of chocolate, how absolutely scrumptious!" Mrs Bugglepuff couldn't resist and she stuck her tongue out and gave the door frame a big lick and laughed. "Oh, and it's really very good chocolate, too. But where is Seasea?"

She slowly opened the door to be hit by a blaze of pink walls.

A glittering pink piano sat near the doorway with pink and purple keys, and a pink satin stool with pearls threaded around the edges. There was a dressing room beyond the piano full of every type of sparkly, pink, shimmering dress you could ever imagine. All had matching shoes with butterfly and fairy wing jewelled ties.

"What a delight!" giggled Mrs Bugglepuff.

A heart-shaped bathroom to the right of the door had – you can guess – a roll top Victorian bath made completely out of chocolate! The rest of the bathroom was sparkling with a pink rhinestone sink, toilet, and a pink glittery floor.

Seasea's main bedroom was round and eighteen feet across. The central feature was the ceiling that rose up into a stained glass turret with a mural depicting magical woodland of primroses and bluebells. There was a mythical pink unicorn with a long, gleaming white mane and tail. It stood by a pink waterfall that flowed down the ceiling and splashed down the wall over a large pink wall map. Exactly the same as Rocky's, but just in pink.

"How marvellous, and magical!" Once again Mrs Bugglepuff was so completely mesmerised by such an inventive imagination that she had to lean against the wall to take it all in.

"Oooow! Yuck! What's this?"

In her hand was a slightly squashed, syrupy, stripy fairy cake with honeycomb crumbs on top. Mrs Bugglepuff picked it up and took a generous bite. The flavours of apricot jam, sponge, dusted sugars, and honeycomb sprinkles were so naughty.

"What a yummy cake," but as she looked down at the empty space there was another and another and another. In fact a glorious band of multi-coloured fairy cakes necklaced around Seasea's bedroom. Pink icing, jelly tots, sparkly ones, spotty fizzy ones, chocolate sprinkles with whipped cream, butterfly candy toppings, rainbow ice cream, candy floss towers, and sugar crystal flower petals cascaded over the edges. Each cake was different from the next and so deliciously tempting.

"A fairy cake shelf in your bedroom, that's every six years olds dream!" Mrs Bugglepuff clapped her hands together with excitement and turned to look at Seasea's new bed – and what a bed!

A large fluffy, round pink cat bed set on a glimmering glass platform. The headrest had a giant smiling cat's face, pink night light eyes and curly whiskers from which hung a variety of sparkling bangles, rings, hair clips and bobbles at the ends. The bottom of the bed had a giant furry pink tail that curled round into a long bouncy, beanbag. It trailed over six feet along the edge of a half-moon pink bookshelf, full of sequined books, sewing and dressing up bibles, books about cooking cupcakes, and fairy tale novels.

Mrs Bugglepuff softly stepped up to the bed and there lying under candyfloss pink satin sheets was Seasea resting her beautiful golden hair on satin pink puffy pillows. Mrs Bugglepuff proudly kissed Seasea's forehead and she woke.

"Mum, Mum, am I dreaming?" she said, as she gazed in sleepy, wide-eyed shock around at her new super pink glittering bedroom.

"No, my Darling, I think I'm in your dream. What a beautiful room you've made!"

"You explore your new bedroom and I'll go and check on Compass and Anemone. Breakfast in thirty minutes Seasea, ok?"

"Ok! Ok! Wha-hey! Wha-hey! Yippee! Yes, Mum," laughed Seasea as she bounced up and down on her bed that started to purr and purr as she jumped. They both laughed, hugged again, and Mrs Bugglepuff left a thrilled Seasea to explore her new magical room.

CHAPTER EIGHT
INTO THE LION'S DEN

Mrs Bugglepuff's head was suddenly exploding with the dramatic room changes; and as she left Seasea, she paused to quietly sit on a lone rocking chair halfway along the corridor.

"I can do this. I can. Come on Mrs Bugglepuff, you must keep going, you must!" Closing her eyes she prepared herself for what lay ahead in Compass and Anemone's rooms. Humming to herself, she rocked gently to calm her pounding heart.

"So where do you want to go next?"

"Who said that? Who said that?" Mrs Bugglepuff turned left and then right but nothing else was in the hallway – nothing but the tick, tick, ticking of the clocks.

"I did, of course. Rocky also dreamt about me. A talking, travelling rocking chair and here I am. Cool, eh?"

"What?" The hairs flew up on Mrs Bugglepuff's back. Her hands went cold as ice and she jumped out of the rocking chair in a flash.

"Hello. I have no name, but you can call me 'Rocky's Rocker'. So, where do you want to go next?" The crest at the top of the rocking chair detailed a blue whale and the whale's mouth was moving.

"So, if I sit on you, you can take me along to Compass' bedroom?" quizzed a giddy Mrs Bugglepuff shaking her head.

"No problem. Take a seat and off we go!"

So, gently she sat back in the rocking chair giving the briefest of smiles at the whale before – *WHOOOOOOOO OOOOOOOOOOOOSH* – and there she was outside another strange door.

"Oh, err, thank you," she laughed.

And – *WHOOOOOOOOOOOOOOOOOOOOOOOOSH* – it was back down the corridor between Seasea's and Rocky's bedroom doors.

"Ok, talking rocking chairs, pirate bedrooms, and crazy cat beds, no problem – what next?"

Surely nothing more could surprise her as she thought about the small box room she had left Compass sleeping in the night before. His grey door was replaced with a heavy-framed door made of bamboo panels tied by coarse brown ropes. On his door hung a sign written in precise handwriting; 'KNOCK! ENTER! CLOSE!' With an afterthought of 'thank you' in very small inky pen. Mrs Bugglepuff's heart began to rapidly race. This magical excitement was all too much for her.

"Deep breath, Delirious, deep breath," she muttered as a number of very strange sounds began echoing through the door. "Whatever's in here?" Taking another deep breath, she lifted the bamboo latch and slowly peered into his room. "Compass dear, are you ok?"

Instantly, Mrs Bugglepuff's cheeks were hit by a dry wave of heat. It was like entering a jungle. She could only see giant lush tropical plants in front of her and hear all sorts of bizarre bird and animal noises. She was definitely not in Devon anymore with air this warm, and Compass' room appeared to have no ceiling at all, just blue skies. The strong scent of exotic flowers, tropical plants, and an earthy smell was in the air.

After maybe ten steps forward, walking through a maze of high, overlapping undergrowth, she looked up and there in a clearing, were two giant trees. High up between the trees was a magnificent bamboo tree house with a bamboo winch, ropes, ladders, and secret hatches in the tree trunks. At the foot of the tree was a pride of sleeping golden lions with two giraffes and four zebras grazing nearby. Toucans, giant butterflies, and a variety of colourful macaw parrots flew overhead. A small group of brown monkeys swung from tree to tree, but the oddest thing was Mrs Bugglepuff wasn't nervous of them.

I should be nervous of all these animals, but why aren't I? She questioned.

Suddenly, a rather familiar and haphazard Albert flew into sight, spiralling around Mrs Bugglepuff and screeching, "Come and see! Come and see!"

"Mum, over here!" signalled Compass in rapturous excitement. He was waving frantically and leaning out of his tree house window in a fine pair of safari pyjamas with Captain Bugglepuff's leather telescope under his elbow.

"Mum, there's no reason to be worried."

"I'm not, I think." She puzzled.

"It's just when I woke, and realised that my dream bedroom had come to life I knew I had nothing to fear, nothing at all!"

"How Compass?"

"Because in my dream all the animals that I wanted in my bedroom got on with each other or just slept, like the lions. I have already stroked the lions this morning and fed the giraffes a bowl of apples by hand. How cool is that?"

"Feeding giraffes in your bedroom is very cool, Compass. Cleaning them out is something else!" Mrs Bugglepuff grinned, rolling her eyes in despair.

"I think my door must stay closed because if the animals were to leave they may change but here they are safe. Come up! Come up and see my dream tree house and all the views. It's amazing!" he waved jumping up and down.

Mrs Bugglepuff tiptoed passed the sleeping lions, and nervously chuckled in disbelief while grabbing her skirt hem as she sat uncomfortably on a bamboo weaved seat. Mrs Bugglepuff hated heights. She didn't mind the lions, but hated heights! Compass slowly began to turn the lever to take her up to his tree house bedroom.

At first Mrs Bugglepuff just stared anxiously down at the sleeping lions. Focussing her attention on one thing seemed the best idea instead of the ever-increasing gap between the ground and the treehouse.

"It's over forty feet above the jungle floor, Mum."

"Oh joy of joys!" murmured Mrs Bugglepuff feeling a wave of nausea growing in her stomach, as she tightly held onto the sides of the seat and closed her eyes to steady her delirious nerves.

Then there was a flash – a light caught her half-closed eyes and she anxiously looked. There before her was a spectacular far-reaching jungle stretching for miles and miles.

"Wow, Compass! How far does your bedroom go?"

"Not far, Mum. It's mostly a painted mural, but it looks very real. If I try and go beyond the river, there's a wall and the sky's just a painted ceiling with clouds. Albert flew up there and knocked his head five times this morning, poor parrot, but the view is still amazing, don't you think?"

"Well yes, it's remarkable."

At the top of the winch, Mrs Bugglepuff took hold of Compass' sweaty hand and stepped on to a bamboo terrace. "Oh Compass, you are a clever boy!"

Inside, there was a long corridor of bamboo shelves stretching for nearly fifteen metres packed with shelf upon shelf of exotic world books on places, animals, climates, and history. Mrs Bugglepuff walked in wonder passed the shelves, taking two grey pebble steps down, and there, suspended between two branches, was Compass' king-sized hammock. Draped over it was the brightest, multi-coloured fleece blanket covered in flying macaws and sumptuous piles of tropical animal-shaped pillows.

Compass raced in and jumped on his bed. "Mum, look at this!" He smiled broadly and whistled loudly. A scattering of leaves blew in through the window followed by ten blue, red, and green macaws, who happily sat on the branches next to his hammock.

"Amazing!" laughed Mrs Bugglepuff taking a calming seat on a bamboo chair. She briefly looked behind it to make sure it didn't move or talk; but thankfully, unlike Rocky's Rocker in the hallway, it was just an ordinary chair and nothing more! She smiled happily at Compass then glanced around at the rest of the room. He had a coconut wood wash bowl in one corner and his clothes were already neatly folded on bamboo shelves.

And then, there it was again. Compass also had the same old map as Rocky and Seasea. This time she noticed a word repeated over and over again sewn in golden thread into the edge 'periculo aqua, periculo aqua.'

"What does that mean?"

"The map, I don't know. It wasn't in my dream so I don't know why it's here!"

"Hmmm" they both thought for a moment, but then Albert fell off his bamboo perch and the moment was lost.

"Mmm, well, it's an incredible room. Your brother and sisters will be so excited when they see it – as will you be when you see theirs. "I can't take this all in. It's quite a shock."

Get dressed now and I'll check on Anemone and (with a worried pause) her room.

"Mum, take the door at the end."

Compass guided Mrs Bugglepuff to a wall with a cleverly hidden panel that swivelled round. A 180 degree turn and there she was back in the first floor corridor.

"Compass, please be careful and come downstairs for breakfast soon and we'll have the Big Bugglepuff Breakfast for a treat, because I think we're all going to need it today."

The Big Bugglepuff Breakfast was made up of everything: bacon, bubble and squeak (potatoes and cabbage pancakes), three varieties of sausages, tomatoes, pancakes with Anemone's syrup, eggs – scrambled, fried, and boiled – buttered mushrooms, and Delirious' special homemade Bugglepuff ketchup.

"Excellent, super excellent, Mum. I'll be down in ten minutes."

She gave him a humongous Bugglepuff hug and walked across the corridor past the softly rocking, rocking chair that hummed, "See you later," and towards the last bedroom belonging to Anemone.

As she crossed the corridor, Mrs Bugglepuff felt uneasy. Anemone's door was made of spectacular silver shells and it was over seven feet tall. The door frame was engraved with images of the sea and galloping horses. It had a hypnotic glow which, for the first time that morning, genuinely frightened her. *I must focus on Anemone, not myself,* she considered.

Mrs Bugglepuff took a cautious step back, then firmly grabbed the regal horse-shaped door handle and began to turn it. Bang! The shutters at the end violently blew open and an icy breeze blew along the corridor. Mrs Bugglepuff was shaken and paused to catch her breath. Then a welcome happy voice echoed up the staircase.

"Darling, Delirious, Can you come downstairs, now!"

Mrs Bugglepuff looked at Anemone's door. Surely Anemone wouldn't have dreamt about anything too bad. She's probably just sleeping in after working so hard yesterday unpacking the car."

Mrs Bugglepuff decided to recover in the kitchen with a cuppa and her Captain before investigating the fourth and final bedroom and what mysterious dreams lay within.

"Well, my dear Captain, you have never seen bedrooms like the children's, not in your wildest dreams."

But as she turned through the archway into the kitchen her jaw dropped and she fell against the wall in dismay.

"So sorry, my love," stuttered an excited and childlike Captain Bugglepuff, who had a large mouthful of profiteroles oozing out of his mouth whilst he tried unsuccessfully to hide a platter of over fifty towering chocolate and cream buns behind his back.

The kitchen looked more like a grand refectory hall. There was a table over thirty feet in length full of every variety of food, flavour, pudding, pie, crumble, cake, pizza, and pickle you could imagine. There were starters, main courses, desserts galore, and one very happy Captain Bugglepuff who was gloriously grazing along the edges.

"NO, NO, NO!" exploded Mrs Bugglepuff.

"You dreamt not about a bedroom, but a kitchen full of food, didn't you? Please dear, this is simply too much. I love you and I love all this food, but I've got a pirate ship, a giant pink cat bedroom, a talking rocking chair, and a tree house in the jungle to cope with upstairs plus all sorts of exotic animals and goodness knows what's in Anemone's room. Please Captain, we have to have one normal room in the house and it has to be the kitchen, *my* kitchen. Where's Skylark, Puffin, Magpie, or Nutter?"

"We're here!" warbled Nutter gliding skilfully above a giant chocolate cake, skimming the sticky chocolate icing off with his hands.

"Geronimo!" shouted Puffin, diving head first into a cream trifle and popping out covered in fruit and custard."

"NO, NO, NO! Please, can you put the kitchen back to normal? This is just too much magic for me. Well apart from that delicious strawberry tart, and that giant steak pie and mash, and maybe also that bowl of toffee meringues. Yes that's it, apart from them, please put my table back to normal and the room size, it's just too much."

"Fine, as you wish," smiled Skylark who'd glided in through the kitchen window to see Nutter and Puffin larking around.

And with a glittering stamp of the boots, the kitchen was back to normal apart from the delicious looking syrupy strawberry tart, the piping hot puff pastry steak pie, the tongue tingling toffee meringues, and yes, Captain

Bugglepuff's badly hidden platter of chocolate and cream buns!

Captain Bugglepuff looked somewhat grumpy but was resolved to enjoy the last remaining delights on the kitchen table.

"Oh good, what a relief!" sighed Mrs Bugglepuff.

"Oh dear!" grumbled Captain Bugglepuff. Who had regretfully lost the opportunity to indulge in food all year long.

"Sorry dear. Now I'm going to make a deliciously tremendous Big Bugglepuff Breakfast this morning."

"With all the trimmings," drooled Captain Bugglepuff.

"Yes, Captain, with all the trimmings," beamed Mrs Bugglepuff who loved to see the Captain's endless enjoyment of food; mostly!

"But I must check on Anemone first. I'm worried about her."

"Ah, Anemone, I think she just raced outside to feed the animals. She's already up."

"Oh, ok. I must go and see her."

"Delirious, what was all that stuff about their bedrooms? Have they changed like ours, and have they met the Guardians yet?"

"My darling Captain, each bedroom is quite extraordinary, literally out of this world, but I don't think the children have met our little Guardians yet! Let's just check on Anemone and I will tell you all about it over a nice cup of tea."

CHAPTER NINE
A REAL BARN DANCE

Anemone came out of the barn rather pale and slightly skittish calling, "Mum, Dad, come quick."

Mrs Bugglepuff looked at the Captain with some alarm as the children never called Captain Bugglepuff 'Dad' unless there was something seriously wrong. They liked calling him Captain and he found it rather piratey and amusing.

"Anemone, m'shipmate, what's the matter?"

"Everything, you had better come out."

Mrs Bugglepuff rapidly retied her apron the right way round, grabbed Captain Bugglepuff's hand, and briefly glanced back at the intriguing entrance gate before briskly turning into the garden.

"What is it, Anemone?" called the Captain.

But they stopped dead in their tracks. What had once been a fairly sparse array of overgrown flowers around Spring Mill yesterday had been transformed into bountiful blooms stretching as far as the eye could see.

"Goodness. Goodness glory be!"

"Yes indeed," said Magpie and Nutter zooming off in their golden boots, "We worked all night to get Spring Mill back into its original state."

The mill stream was dotted with large, glossy lily pads.

Captain Bugglepuff shook his head in amazement at the garden's growth, and, of course, the sight of the little Guardian children whizzing around was simply tremendous! Skylark and Magpie were carrying bags of flower seeds. Puffin was tending to the stream and smiled happily while assisting a rather fat frog onto a lily pad. This tickled the Captain and he turned to Mrs Bugglepuff.

"Pinch me, Delirious … OUCH!"

"Well, you did say to pinch you!" giggled Mrs Bugglepuff at the miraculous changes.

"Remarkable! It's quite remarkable. We're truly in a world of magic!"

Captain Bugglepuff then caught sight of the Bugglepuff car.

It was brand new and immaculate! Not a scratch, not a smudge of chocolate or sandwich crust embedded in the upholstery, "My car. It's perfect!"

Nutter, covered in dirt, grease, and a cube of mouldy cheese on his golden boot shot up from under the car, "Yes, Captain Bugglepuff, that was a very big job, even for magic!"

"It's truly tremendous. Look at it Delirious, sparkling. Thank you my dear fellow. You'd make an excellent shipmate, Nutter," said the Captain proudly.

"Thank you, Captain," said Nutter as he saluted to the Captain, who nodded cheerfully before scooting off to the creek.

Meanwhile, Mrs Bugglepuff had marched ahead.

"Wait for me, Delirious. I'm finding this all a bit much to take in."

The Captain caught up with Mrs Bugglepuff by the oak. Its trunk was swathed with a garland of cowslips and primroses. They looked up at its grand branches and softly blowing leaves before stepping across to the barn. The big red barn had big red doors and was near Rocky's make believe pirate island and next to another ever-winding hillside track leading up to an invitingly dark forest.

"Anemone, dear, you look pale and in such a shocking state."

She was scuffing her pink shoes against the earth and playing frantically with her pigtails.

"What is it? What's the matter?"

"I think I'm going mad. I think I'm going truly mad. It's the barn, in the barn!" Bursting into tears and throwing her arms first around Mrs Bugglepuff, and then firmly around Captain Bugglepuff.

Mrs Bugglepuff took a deep breath, kissed Anemone on the head, rolled up her sleeves, and opened the barn door swiftly. And there were all the animals. They were all lined up in and around the stalls. She registered them one by one.

Polly pig was woofunting her way through her breakfast in her normal messy fashion. The three lovely hens were scattered around the barn, eating their daily mash blissfully unaware of the Guardian Skylark, who was grooming their feathers. Tinks had found a generous pile of hay in the hay loft and was stretched out with just her furry paws in sight. Last but not least, Trooper was patiently waiting for Polly pig to empty her bowl so he could lick it clean.

"Well, yes. Obviously the Guardians were out of the ordinary for the children, but nothing else was different. Well, apart from their bedrooms, and the garden, too. Yes it's probably got on top of Anemone, poor girl."

Mrs Bugglepuff had now got used to seeing these four tiny children racing around in their golden boots and found them completely delightful and rather reassuring in this strange new world. Anemone must have got into a panic about when she saw Skylark in the barn. She smiled and turned to open the red barn door.

"You know, I could do with some more broccoli ends in my breakfast."

Mrs Bugglepuff abruptly stepped back, turning sharply round in a trice. "What? Who said that?" She glanced erratically back around the dusty barn.

"Me!" She looked down and Polly was looking straight back at her.

"Polly? Polly? Was that you?" she half laughed in disbelief and sat down next to her, rubbing her cuddly furry, ginger chin. "Polly Pig, did you just speak to me?"

"Yes, of course I did. We can talk to you now and you can talk to us. One of you dreamed about talking animals last night so now there's no language barrier between humans and animals at Spring Mill."

Mrs Bugglepuff stumbled back on her knees shaking excitedly.

"Oh my! I've always wanted to have a conversation with a pig, how thrilling!"

She began to roll around on the straw floor with laughter and started to babble very fast, just in case they only had so long to talk before she'd wake up from this crazy dream.

"Oh Polly, my gorgeous gorgeous pig. You are a delight; and the way you look after Seasea is magnificent. I've always wanted to say that and now I can. Oh, how puddingly glorious you are!" Mrs Bugglepuff tickled and tickled Polly pig until Polly was lying on her side gigglunting and gigglunting.

"What about me?" a strong earthy accent echoed behind Mrs Bugglepuff.

"Oh Trooper! You too, how nice to meet you, and thank you for guarding my dear Captain Bugglepuff. How brave you are aboard the boat in those stormy seas. Oh, the Captain is going to be thrilled. I must get him. Wait. Wait here."

Nearly ten minutes had elapsed since Mrs Bugglepuff had first entered the barn alone. There was a firm thump from the big barn door.

"Mum," followed by "Delirious. Are you alright?"

Mrs Bugglepuff came out covered in straw, bubbling with tears and hysterical energy, "Alright? I am more than alright."

By now Rocky, Compass, and Seasea had also made their way outside to meet the new Spring Mill, the magical blossoms and the Guardians, who were happily introducing themselves to the Bugglepuff children.

"Children, Captain Bugglepuff," she paused to take a very deep and exhilarating breath, "I'd like you to meet our family pets. *Really* meet our family pets."

She swung open the barn doors and there they all were. For a second the children looked confused by their mad mother.

"Hi Rocky, where are we off to today? Let's make another treasure map and climb a cliff!" rasped Haphazard, Bolt, and Snowball, the hens.

"Seasea, do you want to collect the eggs and play hide and seek around the garden?" chortled Polly Pig with half a carrot still dangling from the edge of her mouth, as she wiggled her furry, piggy tail in play.

"I could really do with a scratch on my back, Captain," remarked Trooper as he bounded out of the barn planting his paddy paws firmly on top of his master's feet.

The children and Captain were amazed. Stunned, to be precise! Then it clicked and there was mass babbling, hugging, and kissing in all directions from the Bugglepuffs and their pets.

"Oh this is just too tremendous for words!"

Mrs Bugglepuff was almost out of puff with her new family life. She stroked the pets, kissed her husband and blew a kiss to the children.

"I think I'll go and make the Big Bugglepuff Breakfast!"

Unravelling her muddled magical thoughts, she strolled past Magpie to the house, remarking, "Please no more surprises. Today I'm quite surprised out!"

"No, no more today, but maybe tomorrow," laughed Magpie, who zipped off after Compass and Albert to the water's edge.

Back inside, she paused briefly at the bottom of the staircase, tapping her fingers nervously on the wall. Her thoughts floated back to Anemone's bedroom, but since she was outside there couldn't be anything too bad in it so she simply turned into the kitchen.

The kitchen was spotless. Skylark had finished with the hens and was already helping to prepare the Big Bugglepuff Breakfast and had made a welcome cup of tea, white, one sugar for Mrs Bugglepuff's frazzled mind.

She felt inside her apron pocket. The Spring key was warmly resting there. She patted it comfortingly and listened with delight to the Bugglepuff's chatter streaming through the windows. A truly fine adventure had begun!

CHAPTER TEN
TROUBLE AT MILL

A week had passed and everyone and everything had settled into their new magical world and quirky routines. It was calm, almost too calm. No Bugglepuff squabbles or teasing between the children. It had been a very happy week, indeed, thought Mrs Bugglepuff. Suddenly, pop – the bubble had burst. Anemone stormed past the kitchen window in floods of tears.

"What's the matter? What on earth's the matter, Anemone?"

Her sobs, as she turned and ran upstairs, could be heard all over the mill.

"Well, oh dear me, all change!" sighed Mrs Bugglepuff to Puffin who had been organising the Bugglepuff's kitchen cupboards.

Mrs Bugglepuff always dealt with family problems of any kind head on. Like when Rocky threw a tantrum and deliberately knocked a bubbling pot of porridge over. Mrs Bugglepuff then chased him and his chickens with a wooden spoon through the streets of Brixham scolding, "You will come home and you will tidy up all the porridge you've deliberately dropped, Rocky. It's all over my kitchen floor and me, you rascal!" The Brixham neighbours heard plenty from the Bugglepuff house. Mainly to their own amusement when one of the children or a pet had got into a pickle over something.

Anemone was normally the one to reassure her Mum, so Mrs Bugglepuff felt a little apprehensive when she reached the top of the stairs. Knocking softly and feeling an icy chill in the air, Mrs Bugglepuff entered.

"Anemone, Anemone dear. Are you ok?"

"Come in, Mum," sobbed Anemone. Mrs Bugglepuff hadn't been in her room until now. Anemone's room, like the others, was much larger but felt colder and less inviting for some strange reason.

Inside was the most dramatic deep blue mosaic mural of the sea detailing Anemone swimming in Brixham Bay. Jagged diamond encrusted waves were crashing around the edges of the far walls. The sea spilled over dazzling the floor and ceiling, and there pounding out of the water was a magnificent gleaming golden horse, with a long glistening, black, flowing mane and tail. The horse had deep, commanding emerald green eyes and a penetrating glare.

Mrs Bugglepuff shivered and the key in her pocket seemed to tingle sensing something fearful in his presence. Placing her hands firmly back in her apron pockets, she brushed away her own worried thoughts, and turned swiftly towards Anenome.

And there was Anemone on her bed which was quite different to the one she'd seen a week ago. It was seven feet by seven feet with two fearsome, galloping horses carved into each side of the bed, their muscular legs raising the bed to nearly three feet off the floor. This was a dream horse bed by any stretch of the imagination and simply a work of art.

Mrs Bugglepuff clambered onto the bed to stroke Anemone's tear sodden face. "Dear Anemone, nothing can be that bad surely. What's wrong?"

"Mum, it's just that everyone else has a pet, and I know I have Tinks, but I've always wanted a pony and the boys were teasing me about it. Can't I get one?"

"Those naughty, naughty boys, hmm! My dear, look, we've just moved. There have been a lot of unexplainable and fabulous changes. Give us a little while to settle in to all this magic and then we'll see. Yes, we have the land, dearest Anemone, but I must speak to the Captain first, ok?"

"I understand," groaned Anemone, but she felt very angry with her brothers for teasing her. She gave Mrs Bugglepuff a brief hug, wiped her eyes, and slumped off the bed back to the garden.

Rocky had been joined by Nutter and they'd disappeared over the hillside with the hens clutching treasure maps and pirate flags in their beaks.

Compass, Magpie, and Puffin were on the edge of the creek fishing with Albert, who was squawking, "I can fly. You can hear. I can fly. We are here."

Seasea, Skylark, and Polly were dancing around the apple orchard in the far meadow and Tinks, as lovely as she was, preferred to sleep on the kitchen window ledge and bask in the sun purring, "Oh life is so hard for me. Where to sleep next, under a tree or in the barn? It's such a big decision. I am purrfection," she beamed with a wide whiskered smile.

Anemone briefly smiled back at Tinks, stroking her chin. "Yes, my beautiful tabby. You are purrfection." But Tinks simply purred back, stretched out her paws and rolled her eyes shut for another extended morning nap.

Anemone sighed. She was feeling uncharacteristically very grumpy, which was unlike her.

Night after night since she arrived at Spring Mill, she'd had dark dreams about the horse depicted in her bedroom. Calling to her again and again but she didn't know why she was so drawn to it.

It was all too much and she decided to try and clear her thoughts of this dream horse by exploring the endlessly winding creek path. She wandered along listening to the sounds of birds and the lapping water's edge, climbing under and over fallen tree branches and across muddy grass banks.

Then, as she turned a corner, she spotted a rather overgrown building up ahead. It was an abandoned boathouse on a sheltered bank. *That looks interesting*, she thought. She wondered if she should call the others. She decided not to since they'd been mean. *I'll tell them about it later when I've finished exploring it*, she considered.

The boathouse was on two storeys, made of cobbled grey stone. The roof had collapsed on the right and was furiously overgrown with ivy, but you could access the front of it by stepping across a series of large, jagged rocks to a precariously fragile wooden jetty. This gave Anemone direct access to the deep water's edge.

"Maybe I'll have a swim. That always makes me feel better," she remarked out loud. She stepped up onto the creaking wooden jetty, and for some minutes tried to look through the boarded up windows into the blank darkness of the boathouse.

"Boring, absolutely nothing to see in there."

Anemone glanced down, and in amongst the ivy was something jutting out. She pulled and pulled until eventually the vines broke away and there was an old pump handle with a striking horse's head on it. *Intriguing, Rocky would love this discovery,* Anemone thought.

"Wow!" Anemone found a grubby, tear sodden tissue in her pocket and began to gently wipe the moss-covered horse head. One, two, three, four strokes, then suddenly the wooden jetty began to shake and break up. The wooden jetty boards were loosening in every direction; the nails were unpinning and flying about. Anemone tried desperately to leap from board to board but lost her footing and plunged into the cold creek fully clothed. She was under for no more than a few seconds when she felt something lift her forcefully by her hoodie from the water. Thankfully, Anemone was placed back on land, coughing and spluttering.

She dragged her soaking body from the water and turned to lie on the jetty floor. Something was spraying a warm, fine mist of water across her face and neck. At first, the sun blinded her, but then she saw him, the most magnificent horse rearing up on the water's edge. He towered above her, his coat gleaming against the sun, with a jet black flowing mane and tail. Anemone was possessed, truly possessed by his majesty.

"Anemone, I am the King of the Water Horses. My name is Zephorous. I have been trapped in this pump by the

Guardians of Spring Mill for so long!" He raised his gleaming powerful front hoof above her to strike, but paused, setting it down firmly on the pebbled creek.

"You know the Guardians aren't to be trusted!" he thundered, piercing his fierce green eyes into Anemone's soul.

Anemone shuddered. She was still getting used to her strange new bedroom, talking pets, little Guardians, but a speaking horse was just a dream come true, Anemone's dream.

He was dangerous and had a fearsome gaze, but Anemone blanked these concerns for now.

"You're on my wall, in my bedroom and my dreams!"

"Yes, Anemone, yes, I've been waiting for you – for you, Anemone!"

His tone was deep, empowering, and hypnotic.

"Waiting for me?" Anemone glowed with excitement.

"Yes. It's not just by chance that you have found me. It's your destiny, our destiny!" Zephorous pounded the ground with his hooves and lowered his golden neck to look deeper into Anemone's besotted eyes.

"So Anemone, how can I repay you? I am indebted to you."

After a slight hesitation, "A ride?"

"Speak up child." Zephorous motioned with a flick of his glossy black mane.

"Would you take me on a ride? That's what I wish for!"

"So be it, Anemone. For one day I will come out of the water and you can ride me. We shall canter over the hills and jump the highest jumps, but then I must return to the water's edge."

He bent his front legs down and she swung onto his back. With a magical force, Anemone and Zephorous were off.

Galloping, jumping from field to field, Anemone was enraptured with Zephorous's speed, stride, and enduring pace as she gripped onto his powerful neck. Time flew by and the midday sun slowly faded as sunset came too soon. They walked gently back along the creek to the boathouse talking softly with Anemone's arms wrapped around Zephorous' mane.

All too soon, Anemone begrudgingly slid off his back and stroked him one last time. He bowed his head towards her and almost forgot his purpose for a moment. Then, with a refreshed and ever-commanding gaze, he looked sharply back at Anemone and asked, "Anemone, would you like to see me again?"

"Again, oh Zephorous, yes!" exclaimed Anemone in star-struck awe.

"Tomorrow, I will be here at noon, but you must do something for me."

"Anything, anything at all!" pledged Anemone.

"You must bring me the Spring key to Spring Mill," instructed Zephorous.

"The Spring key? Why?"

"I only want to borrow it," and after a pause, he added, "for a while."

"Ok. Twelve, twelve noon," Anemone repeated and repeated.

And with that Zephorous reared up and was gone into the depths of the river Dart with a thunderous roar.

Anemone was in her element, no one had seen her riding, and no one had seen a thing. She beamed with a secretive smile all the way home. Compass, Magpie, and Puffin had long since given up fishing, and Mrs Bugglepuff was ringing the bell for dinner.

She skipped in to a full table of eagle eyes looking back at her.

"Where have you been, m'shipmate?" questioned Captain Bugglepuff.

"Yes, where have you been?" quizzed Seasea.

"Oh, here and there, just getting my bearings."

"Your bearings!" said Rocky and Nutter.

Anenome glared at Nutter thinking to herself '*not to be trusted*', but Nutter had darted off to the garden before he could catch her piercing stare.

"Mmm," Compass was less than convinced, and if truth be known, neither was Mrs Bugglepuff. But since the whole family was now back together, she brushed further questions under the rug for now.

The children finished their supper in superfast time and yawned all the way up to their new, rather more theatrical, dream bedrooms.

Anemone was the last to gently close her bedroom door and settle down to sleep with a sickly excitement growing inside.

"Tomorrow, I will see the King of the Water Horses. Goodnight, Zephorous," murmured Anemone wishfully.

"Goodnight, Anemone," echoed Zephorous.

"Zephorous?" she flinched but was too tired to look around her dimly lit bedroom anymore. Turning over on her warm pillow, she softly closed her eyes, mumbling, "Tomorrow, I must get the Spring key from Mum's pocket."

EPILOGUE

The TPOT tea rooms had nearly emptied. "Well, young man, look at the time, I really must be going. I've taken up all your afternoon, you've been very kind to listen to my story," chuckled the old lady as she reached for her clutch purse.

"What! What! What do you mean, you can't leave it there. You can't just stop. I have used up three pencils, and two notepads." I was looking thoroughly desperate and was eager for more!

"What happens next? What happens to Anemone, the pets, the family and that Magic Key? This will make a glorious first feature for me in the Herald Express."

"Oh my dear boy, you really have entered the world of the Bugglepuffs."

"Well, of course, so…?"

"So, I must be going, but every Tuesday I take a stroll around Brixham harbour. There is a rickety bench in a garden near Berry Head which has some of the most glorious sea views, you'll find me there shortly before ten but gone by eleven."

Gracefully she rose. I had no time to utter anymore disappointing objections and closed my notebook for now. She patted my hand softly, re-fixed her sunflower hairpin; beamed a warm smile, and left the silly TPOT tea rooms assisted by her very curiously shaped walking stick.

BUGGLEPUFF
GLORIOUS THANKS

My family and crazy pets for their love, laughter in creating the world of the Bugglepuffs and for the hilarious day to day inspiration they give me.

Bob, Tom, Ginny, Dan, Andrew, Kevin, Jaime, Rebecca, Dwain and all the publishing team, a big thank you for your guidance, patience and amazing Bugglepuff support!

To Steve, Rob and Kayleigh for their website wonders and magical designs!

Tremendous thanks to the children and adults who are reading the book and joining the world of the Bugglepuffs with me! It's going to be quite an adventure!

See you soon C L BENNETT.

Bugglepuffs and the Magic Key

by C.L. Bennett